For Sophie

Text and illustrations copyright © 2009 by Ingrid and Dieter Schubert
Originally published under the title *Olifantensoep* by Lemniscaat b.v. Rotterdam, 2009
All rights reserved
Printed in Belgium
First U.S. edition, 2010

CIP data is available.

Lemniscaat
An Imprint of Boyds Mills Press, Inc.
815 Church Street
Honesdale, Pennsylvania 18431

Ingrid & Dieter Schubert

Elephant Soup

Lemniscaat

HONESDALE, PENNSYLVANIA

Sometimes I feel down in the dumps.
Do you know what I do when that happens?

I gather my friends together . . .

and I bring an enormous pot.

Because when you are feeling blue,
there is only one thing that helps:

elephant soup!

My friends fill the pot with water
and build a fire.

In the meantime, I catch an elephant.

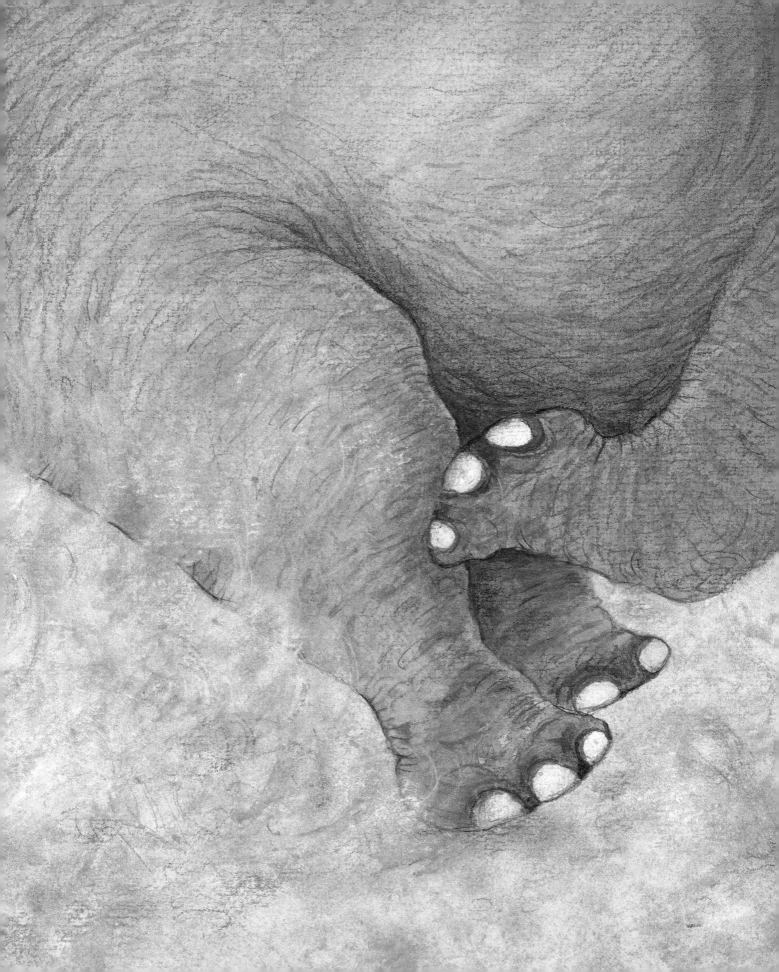

The recipe is simple.
Scrub gently.

Slide the elephant into the pot
and let simmer till nice and pink.

Add your favorite vegetables.
Season with salt and pepper.
Place the lid on the pot.

Now it's ready.

Stop! A lid?!
The elephant is too big!

Now what?
No soup!

But we still have the pot.

And fortunately, we have the elephant!